The Elf Who Lived Next Door

Written by Bill and
Illustrated by

"Our neighbor is an elf," Melissa whispered.

"Who? Mr. Short?" her older brother said. "Grow up, Melissa. He's just a friendly old man who used to run a toy company."

A toy company. Yup. That's what elves do, Melissa thought.

It was the day before Christmas. Mr. Short was called out of town on a sudden business trip.

He asked the children to feed his guppies. "Here's the key to my house," he said, and handed it to Melissa.

A key to an elf's house, Melissa thought. Wow!

"We're only here to feed the guppies," her brother reminded her. But as they climbed the porch steps to Mr. Short's house, Melissa couldn't wait to see inside.

Inside everything was cozy, warm and wonderful.
It even smelled like gingerbread and cinnamon.

"*Exactly the way an elf's house should smell,*"
Melissa thought.

Then Melissa spotted the framed photo of Santa Claus on the mantlepiece.Santa was outside next to his sleigh, with snow falling all around him. You could almost feel the cold air.

The photo was signed — "To Shorty, Love Santa."

To Shorty,
Love, Santa

Melissa stood on her tiptoes and stared at the
picture. Then she slowly backed away and bumped
right into a rocking chair. That's when she noticed the
red velvet slippers with pointy toes that curled up at
the ends and two little silverbells on each tip.

"They look like Santa elf slippers!" Melissa said out loud. On the word *Santa* the slipper's bells tinkled the tiniest, sweetest "Jingle Bells."

"Joe! Joe! Come see the elf shoes!" Melissa shouted.

Joe looked at the shoes. He watched while
Melissa said *Santa* and the slippers tinkled Jingle Bells.
"They're magic, right?" Melissa said.

Joe shook his head. "Nah. They're just another voice activated music box gismo," he said.

"You don't know the first thing about Santa Claus or elves," Joe snapped.

"In fact, if you want to know the truth, there are no such things as elves. Elves are pretend...for little babies like you to believe in."

"And if you want to know the truth I don't believe in Santa Claus at all!" Joe shouted.

"Because," Joe kept talking, "if there was such a thing as Santa, he would have known about that new official basketaball I wanted...and didn't get!"

Melissa couldn't believe what her brother was saying.

"But you got new sneakers ... and all those toys and games..."

"Those were from Mom and Dad, Melissa."

Melissa started to cry.

"Put Mr. Short's slippers back where you found them," Joe said. "And don't talk to me about elves anymore." He was angry. "Come on," he said. "Let's go."

Melissa put the slippers back near the chair. That's
when she noticed a tiny purple silk bag with the words "Magic
Beads" embroidered on it in gold thread.

Melissa opened the bag — just to peek in. The magic
beads were all different colors.

She grabbed a handfull of beads and suddenly heard
a sudden whoosh.

What was happening?
Was she rising up into the air?
Yes! Melissa was floating an inch above the floor.

"Joe! Joe!" she screamed.

By the time Joe ran back in to the room the beads had disappeared and Melissa just stood there holding the little purple bag, with no proof that Mr. Short was an elf.

Suddenly, both children heard a loud thud on the roof. They ran to the window and tried to open it. But it was shut tight. Then there was scraping sound — like the sound of a sleigh — and a stomping sound — like so many hooves — reindeer hooves? And sleigh bells.

Melissa heard the sound of jolly laughter — a Ho!
Ho! Ho! that rolled out happily from someone's big belly.

Melissa looked at Joe. It wasn't her imagination. He
heard it too. Both children stared at each other as they listened
to the muffled words coming from the roof.

A deep voice laughed and said, "Thank you, Shorty! See
you next year!"

The children still had their faces pressed to the window, with their backs to the fireplace. So they didn't see Mr. Short come in.

Melissa was sure he'd come down the chimney while they weren't looking. Joe thought that Mr. Short came through the front door, even though there weren't any footsteps in the suddenly falling snow.

"Hello Joe. Hello Melissa. I'm home! Merry Christmas!"
The sounds on the roof had disappeared with a
whoosh of wind and bells. Now here stood Mr. Short,
apple-cheeked from the cold, holding two big giftwrapped
boxes.

"I've got some merry presents for you both," Mr. Short chuckled.

"Just let me get my cold boots off, and put some hot cocoa on the stove. Then you can open up your gifts."

Mr. Short called from the kitchen, "Joe, your gift is the one in the green box. Melissa, yours is the one in the red box."

In a few seconds flat, Mr. Short was back with a tray of steaming hot cocoa.

"Well, go ahead. Open your presents!"

Melissa wanted to open her gift carefully. The wrapping paper was so beautiful. But she had to see what was inside and the only way to do that was to rip the paper – and open the box and – oooh! It was the ice skates she had dreamed about.

"Look Joe," she said.

But Joe was staring at his own gift. There, nestled in tissue paper inside the big square box was an offical regulation professional basketball – exactly what he had hoped for.

"It's exactly what we wanted, Mr. Short," said the children. "I know," Mr. Short winked.

"Uh, Melissa," Joe said softly, "Forget what I said about elves being pretend, okay?"

Melissa smiled at her brother.

"And forget what I said about Santa, too."

On the word *Santa* the two red velvet slippers tinkled *Jingle Bells Jingle Bells Jingle all the way....*

And both children smiled at their neighbor, Mr. Short.